NO LONGER PROPERTY OF
GLENDALE LIBRARY ARTS
& CULTURE DEPT.

CHILDREN'S ROOM

S0-BTS-203

POISONOUS PLANTS

by Mari Schuh

pogo

j 581.659 SCH

Ideas for Parents and Teachers

Pogo Books let children practice reading informational text while introducing them to nonfiction features such as headings, labels, sidebars, maps, and diagrams, as well as a table of contents, glossary, and index.

Carefully leveled text with a strong photo match offers early fluent readers the support they need to succeed.

Before Reading

- "Walk" through the book and point out the various nonfiction features. Ask the student what purpose each feature serves.
- Look at the glossary together. Read and discuss the words.

Read the Book

- Have the child read the book independently.
- Invite him or her to list questions that arise from reading.

After Reading

- Discuss the child's questions. Talk about how he or she might find answers to those questions.
- Prompt the child to think more. Ask: Did you know about poisonous plants before reading this book? What more would you like to learn about them?

Pogo Books are published by Jump!
5357 Penn Avenue South
Minneapolis, MN 55419
www.jumplibrary.com

Copyright © 2019 Jump!
International copyright reserved in all countries.
No part of this book may be reproduced in any form without written permission from the publisher.

Library of Congress Cataloging-in-Publication Data

Names: Schuh, Mari C., 1975- author.
Title: Poisonous plants / by Mari Schuh.
Description: Minneapolis, MN : Jump!, Inc., [2018]
Series: Plant power
"Pogo Books are published by Jump!"
Audience: Ages 7-10.
Includes bibliographical references and index.
Identifiers: LCCN 2017061421 (print)
LCCN 2017057196 (ebook)
ISBN 9781624968853 (ebook)
ISBN 9781624968839 (hardcover : alk. paper)
ISBN 9781624968846 (pbk.)
Subjects: LCSH: Poisonous plants—Juvenile literature.
Plant defenses—Juvenile literature.
Classification: LCC QK100.A1 (print)
LCC QK100.A1 S38 2018 (ebook) | DDC 581.6/59—dc23
LC record available at https://lccn.loc.gov/2017061421

Editor: Jenna Trnka
Book Designer: Molly Ballanger

Photo Credits: Valentina Razumova/Shutterstock, cover; Melinda Fawver/Shutterstock, 1; Potapov Alexander/Shutterstock, 3; Kerrie W/Shutterstock, 4; Cora Niele/Getty, 5; age fotostock/SuperStock, 6-7; Visuals Unlimited, Inc./Gerald & Buff Corsi/Getty, 8-9; alfocome/Shutterstock, 10; Photodynamx/Dreamstime, 11; RukiMedia/Shutterstock, 12-13; Daisuke Nishioka JP/Shutterstock; 14-15; David Cole/Alamy, 16-17; Stefano Paterna/age fotostock/SuperStock, 18; Eye Ubiquitous/SuperStock, 19; Martin Siepmann/imageBROKER/SuperStock, 20-21; Dewin'Indew/Shutterstock, 23.

Printed in the United States of America at Corporate Graphics in North Mankato, Minnesota.

TABLE OF CONTENTS

CHAPTER 1

BAD BERRIES

Green leaves spread out in the shade. These leaves are part of a white baneberry plant. This plant has another name. What is it?

Doll's eyes. Each white berry has a dark spot. These scary berries are **poisonous**.

Shiny black berries grow on the deadly nightshade plant. They look juicy and tasty. But don't be tricked. They are also called devil's berries. Or death cherries. With names like that, you have been warned!

death camas

Poisonous plants use poison as a **defense**. Against what? Animals, such as birds, that try to eat the plant.

Plants can have poison in their berries, leaves, **stems**, or **roots**. Plants such as the death camas have poison in all of their parts.

DID YOU KNOW?

A plant that is poisonous for one animal may not be harmful to another. Poison ivy can give people a rash. But it doesn't harm birds. Birds can even eat the plant's fruit.

CHAPTER 2

HARMFUL PLANTS

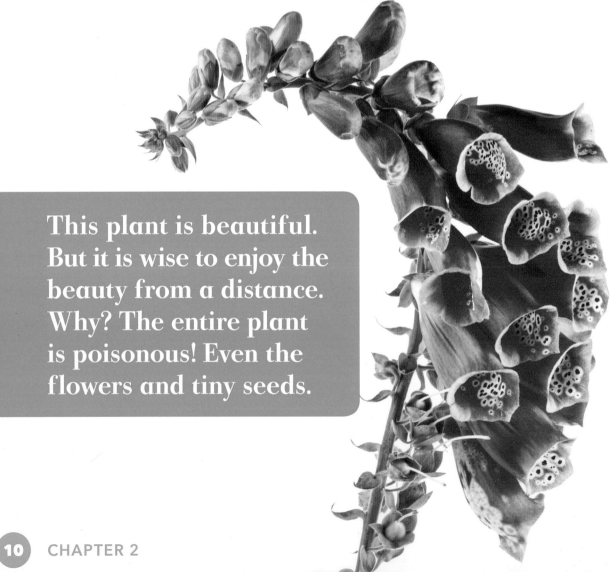

This plant is beautiful. But it is wise to enjoy the beauty from a distance. Why? The entire plant is poisonous! Even the flowers and tiny seeds.

This plant is the foxglove. It is also called bloody fingers and witch's gloves. It has bell-shaped blossoms. They are usually bright purple. They can be white, yellow, or pink, too. Many private gardens host these beauties.

Beware! Flame lilies warn visitors of their danger. Their bright leaves curl and bend like flames. All parts of this plant are poisonous. Bright colors warn predators that these plants are bad to eat.

What is this unique plant? Its long, floppy leaf folds over the flower. It forms a hood. If you see this plant growing in wet woodlands, don't get too close. It is a jack-in-the-pulpit. All parts of this plant can cause harm. Under the soil, even more danger lurks. The plant's roots contain terrible poison.

DID YOU KNOW?

Poisonous plants can be deadly. But some can be used to make medicine. Chemicals in the poisonous rosy periwinkle plant are used to help fight diseases, for example.

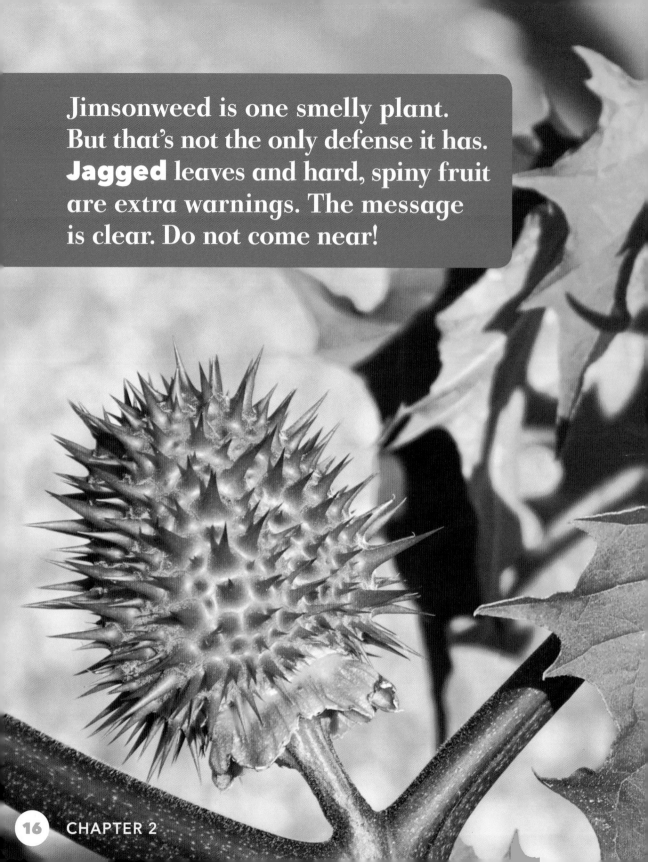

Jimsonweed is one smelly plant. But that's not the only defense it has. **Jagged** leaves and hard, spiny fruit are extra warnings. The message is clear. Do not come near!

TAKE A LOOK!

All parts of the jimsonweed plant are poisonous.

FLOWERS
Large, tube-shaped flowers are usually white or violet. They have a strong odor, giving the plant another name: stinkweed.

STEM
The stem is green and sometimes tinged with violet.

LEAVES
Leaves are large, green, and jagged.

FRUIT
Spiky fruits are also called "thorn apples."

SEEDS
Poisonous black seeds spill from the ripened fruit.

CHAPTER 3

TOXIC TREES AND SHRUBS

Manchineel trees ooze. With what? Poisonous **sap**. It seeps from the tree's bark, leaves, branches, and fruit.

Think you would be safe standing under this **toxic** tree when it rains? Think again! Raindrops mix with the nasty sap. It can cause rashes, blisters, and itching.

DANGER

Fruit from the
Manchineel Tree is
Poisonous.
Handling leaves and fruit may
irritate skin and eyes

oleander

Flowers **bloom** on the oleander **shrub**. They are beautiful. But this is one of the most poisonous plants in the world. So look if you must. But don't touch!

Many poisonous plants are colorful. Vivid colors are a telling sign. The plant is poisonous. Poison keeps these plants safe from predators of all kinds. But they are best seen, not touched.

DID YOU KNOW?

Oleander poison is very strong. How strong? It has shown up in honey made by bees that visit the plant's flowers.

ACTIVITIES & TOOLS

COLOR CHANGES

Berries on the deadly nightshade plant change from green to black as they ripen and get more poisonous. In this activity, watch color changes as bananas ripen in your own kitchen.

What You Need:

- two unripe bananas
- plastic airtight see-through storage container
- pen or pencil
- paper or notebook

1. Put one banana in the airtight container.

2. Keep the other banana on the kitchen counter.

3. For eight days in a row, look closely at each banana. Compare the two bananas. Do you see any changes? Are the bananas changing color?

4. Each day, write the date in your notebook. Also describe each banana. Write about the changes you see.

5. On the last day, write about how each banana changed. Did they change color? Which banana ripened first?

GLOSSARY

bloom: To produce flowers.

defense: A way to protect from harm or attack.

jagged: Sharp and uneven.

poisonous: Able to harm or kill with a harmful substance.

roots: The parts of a plant or tree that grow under the ground and collect water and nutrients.

sap: A sticky fluid found inside plants and trees.

shrub: A plant or bush with woody stems that spread out near the ground.

stems: The main upward-growing parts of plants from which leaves and flowers grow.

toxic: Poisonous.

INDEX

TO LEARN MORE

Learning more is as easy as 1, 2, 3.

1) Go to www.factsurfer.com

2) Enter "poisonousplants" into the search box.

3) Click the "Surf" button to see a list of websites.

With factsurfer, finding more information is just a click away.